The Berenstain Bears and the MESSY ROOM

When small bears forget
To pick up, store and stash,
Some of their favorite things
End up in the trash.

A FIRST TIME BOOK®

The Berenstain Bears and the MESSY

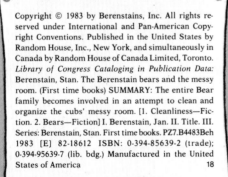

ROOM

Stan & Jan Berenstain

Random House   New York

From the outside, the Bears' tree house, which stood beside a sunny dirt road deep in Bear Country, looked very neat and well-kept.

The flower beds sparkled with red, yellow, and blue tulips.

The woodwork was freshly painted and in good repair.

The grass was cut and the vegetable patch was properly weeded.

Even the bird's nest that perched on one of the tree house branches was well-trimmed.

The inside of the Bears'
tree house was neat and clean too.

The pictures were straight.

The piano was dusted.

The kitchen was spick-and-span.

Even the basement was neat and clean.
(And if you think it's easy to keep a
tree house basement neat and clean—
well, you've never tried to do it!)

Yes, the Bears' tree house was a
lesson in neatness and cleanliness.

Except for one place...

Brother Bear and Sister Bear's room.
IT...WAS...A...*MESS*!!!

A dust-catching, wall-to-wall, helter-skelter mess!

A half-done jigsaw puzzle gathered dust in one corner of the room.

A group of Brother's dinosaur models collected cobwebs in another.

Sister's stuffed animals were everywhere.

It wasn't that Brother and Sister were naturally messy. They *tried* to keep their room straight.

They made their beds...

most of the time,

and they swept
and picked up...

once in a while.

The trouble was that when clean-up time came, they spent more time arguing than cleaning.

"How am *I* supposed to sweep with your dumb dinosaur toys all over the floor?" argued Sister.

"They're not toys—they're *models*! And don't move them! I'm working on a set-up of the Pleistocene Age!" Brother protested.

"Pleistocene schmeistocene!" shouted Sister.

Not only was Brother and Sister's room a mess, but Brother and Sister were getting to be a mess too—always arguing about clean-up chores instead of sharing the job and working as a team.

What usually happened was that while the cubs
argued about whose turn it was to do what,
Mama took the broom and did the sweeping herself…

and she often did the picking up too.
That was the worst part—the picking up.

And the putting away.

Well, the mess just seemed to build up and build up, until one day...maybe it was because Mama's back was a little stiff, or maybe it was stepping on Brother's airplane cement, or maybe she was just fed up with that messy room, but whatever it was...Mama Bear lost her temper!

She stormed into the
cubs' room with a big box.

"The first thing we have to do is get rid of all this junk!" she said.

"JUNK!?" said Brother and Sister, watching in horror as Mama began to throw things into the box.

"My Teddy isn't junk!" screamed Sister.

"My bird's nest collection isn't junk!" yelled Brother at the top of his lungs.

The screaming and yelling got so loud that it reached Papa, who was in his workshop putting the finishing touches on a batch of chairs that had been ordered by one of his customers. He couldn't imagine what was wrong.

He hurried up the stairs and looked into the messy, *noisy* room. It didn't take a deep thinker to figure out what was going on.

QUIET!

Papa got Mama's and the cubs' attention and called a family meeting right then and there.

"Now, the mess has really built up in this room," he said. "In fact, it's the worst case of messy build-up I've ever seen!

"And it isn't fair," he continued. "It isn't fair to your mama and me, because we have a lot of other things to take care of. And it isn't fair to you, because you really can't have fun or relax in a room that's such a terrible mess."

"But Mama is putting all my things into that box—even my Teddy!" said Sister.

"And my things too!" cried Brother. Then Papa got an idea.

"A box, yes," he said. "Better yet, a lot of different kinds of boxes— a big toy box for your large toys... I can make one for you in my shop... and some smaller boxes for your collections and models."

"And how about one of those boards with holes and pegs to hang things on?" asked Sister.

"A pegboard!" said Papa. "Great idea! All this room needs is a little organization."

"A little organization—*and* a few rules!" added Mama. "Rules about more sweeping and less arguing and not leaving things to gather dust and cobwebs."

Papa set to work making
a fine big toy box and a
large pegboard...

while the cubs and Mama
sorted out toys, books, games,
and puzzles and put them
into boxes that fit neatly
into the closet.
Every box was
clearly labeled.

Some of the cubs' things did end up in Mama's big throwaway box—not Sister's Teddy, of course, but some of Brother's bird's nests (the crumbling, falling-apart ones).

It was a very big job cleaning up all that messy build-up. But after a lot of straightening up and putting away, the job was finally finished.

"Wow!" said Brother. "That was quite a job, but it was worth it!"

"It looks like a whole new room!" said Sister.

The cubs were right.

And Papa had been right too. It was so much more enjoyable to live in a neat, clean, well-organized room— and so much more relaxing!

It wasn't as exciting to open the big storage closet now, but it was much more practical—and a lot more fun!